FACT or FICTION?

DO GHOSTS EXIST?

PETER FINN

Gareth Stevens
PUBLISHING

Please visit our website, www.garethstevens.com. For a free color catalog of all our high-quality books, call toll free 1-800-542-2595 or fax 1-877-542-2596.

Library of Congress Cataloging-in-Publication Data

Names: Finn, Peter, 1978- author.
Title: Do ghosts exist? / Peter Finn.
Description: New York : Gareth Stevens Publishing, 2023. | Series: Fact or
    fiction? | Includes index. | Audience: Grades 4-6
Identifiers: LCCN 2021055916 (print) | LCCN 2021055917 (ebook) | ISBN
    9781538280775 (library binding) | ISBN 9781538280751 (paperback) | ISBN
    9781538280768 (set) | ISBN 9781538280782 (ebook)
Subjects: LCSH: Ghosts–Juvenile literature. | Haunted places–Juvenile
    literature.
Classification: LCC BF1461 .F55 2023 (print) | LCC BF1461 (ebook) | DDC
    133.1–dc23/eng/20211209
LC record available at https://lccn.loc.gov/2021055916
LC ebook record available at https://lccn.loc.gov/2021055917

Portions of this work were originally authored by Heather Moore Niver and published as *Are Ghosts Real?*. All new material this edition authored by Peter Finn.

Published in 2023 by
Gareth Stevens Publishing
29 E. 21st Street
New York, NY 10010

Copyright © 2023 Gareth Stevens Publishing

Designer: Sheryl Kober
Editor: Therese Shea

Photo credits: Cover (top) and p. 1 Bubbers BB/Shutterstock.com; cover and p. 1 (middle fire texture) Anna Timoshenko/Shutterstock.com; cover and p. 1 (bottom image) Michal Plachy/Shutterstock.com; pp. 1–32 (web background texture) milart/Shutterstock.com; pp. 1–32 (sidebar background texture) leolintang/Shutterstock.com; back cover and pp. 2–32 (It's A Fact background texture) R_Tee/Shutterstock.com; pp.1–32 (Recto side band) Daniela Illing/Shutterstock.com; p. 3 Susanitah/Shutterstock.com; p. 4 DEL Studio/Shutterstock.com; p. 5 Fotokita/Shutterstock.com; p. 6 Alexander_P/Shutterstock.com; p. 7 Gian Salero/Shutterstock.com; p. 8 alexblacksea/Shutterstock.com; p. 9 MelBrackstone/Shutterstock.com; p. 10 Croisy/Shutterstock.com; p. 11 (top) Valery Sidelnykov/Shutterstock.com; p. 11 (bottom) Croisy/Shutterstock.com; p. 12 carlos 401/Shutterstock.com; p.13 (top) https://en.wikipedia.org/wiki/The_Amityville_Horror#/media/File:Amityville_house.JPG; p. 13 (bottom) Erin Cadigan/Shutterstock.com; p. 14 Sasha_lvv/Shutterstock.com; p. 15 (top) godrick/Shutterstock.com; p. 15 (bottom) Arthur Balitskii/Shutterstock.com; p. 16 Golden Shrimp/Shutterstock.com; p. 17 (top) Hercales Kritikos/Shutterstock.com; p. 17 (bottom) Netfalls Remy Musser/Shutterstock.com; p. 18 Everett Collection/Shutterstock.com; p. 19 (top) Orhan Kam/Shutterstock.com; p. 19 (bottom) Everett Collection/Shutterstock.com; p. 20 (top) Morphart Creation/Shutterstock.com; p. 20 (bottom) Celeste Images/Shutterstock.com; p. 21 (top) Tim Weikert/Shutterstock.com; p. 21 (bottom) Lou Oates/Shutterstock.com; p. 22 Ksenlya Parkhimchyk/Shutterstock.com; p. 23 (top) Joelee Art/Shutterstock.com; p. 23 (bottom) Juiced Up Media/Shutterstock.com; p. 24 Caso Alfonso/Shutterstock.com; p. 25 (top) F-stop boy/Shutterstock.com; p. 25 (bottom) Nazarii_Neshcherenskyi/Shutterstock.com; p. 26 Viktoriia_P/Shutterstock.com; p. 27 https://commons.wikimedia.org/wiki/File:Mumler_(Lincoln).jpg; p. 28 Fine Art/Shutterstock.com; p. 29 (top) Vjacheslav Shishlov/Shutterstock.com; p. 29 (bottom) thanasus/Shutterstock.com.

CPSIA compliance information: Batch #CSGS23: For further information contact Gareth Stevens, New York, New York, at 1-800-542-2595.

Find us on

CONTENTS

Words in the glossary appear in **bold** type the first time they are used in the text.

WAS IT A GHOST?

Have you ever heard, seen, or felt something you couldn't explain? Maybe a strange noise in the night? Perhaps a shadowy figure out of the corner of your eye—that disappears when you turn? What about a sudden, unexplained temperature drop? Some people think these occurrences have an explanation: ghosts.

Ghosts exist in countless stories, books, TV shows, and movies, of course. Some of these spirits are described as evil, while others are good. But many people believe ghosts exist in real life too.

In 2021, a company called YouGov asked 1,000 Americans about ghosts. The survey revealed two in five Americans believe in ghosts. One in five reported they've actually seen a ghost! If you were one of the people surveyed, what would you say?

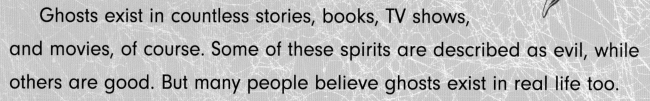

DEFINING A GHOST

Merriam-Webster's Collegiate Dictionary describes a ghost as "the soul of a dead person believed to be an inhabitant [occupant] of the unseen world or to appear to the living in bodily likeness." According to this, ghosts are believed to live in the netherworld, or a place where souls of the dead reside. And some believe ghosts can visit the living too. When they do, they may take a form somewhat like their body.

According to the 2021 YouGov survey, about 41 percent of Americans believe in ghosts, while 39 percent don't believe in them. More women than men reported believing in ghosts.

IT'S A FACT!

The word "ghost" has been used since before the 12th century!

Ghost stories likely came from the idea that human spirits can survive death and live without their physical bodies. Chilling tales of ghosts have been told as far back as recorded history began.

Ancient people told stories of spirits and hauntings. For example, some think a ghost appears in the Old Testament of the Bible in the First Book of Samuel (also called the First Book of Kings). This part of the Bible was written around 550 BCE.

The opening scene in William Shakespeare's play *Hamlet*, which was published in 1603, includes the ghost of a recently dead king. Charles Dickens's story *A Christmas Carol*, published in 1843, features four ghosts in all. Ghost stories have been in popular stories for a long time!

POSSESSION

A possessed person isn't the same as a ghost. Possession means that someone's identity is replaced by an outside identity, often some kind of good or evil spirit. Sometimes unusual behavior is labeled possession. This can include groaning or speaking in a language the person isn't thought to know. Many **cultures** around the world believe in possession. And some also believe in exorcism, or the casting out of a spirit from a person's body.

In the spooky first scene of *Hamlet*, the title character sees the ghost of his dead father.

A **Babylonian** tablet dating back to 1500 BCE may depict, or show, one of the oldest known images of a ghost. Some believe it has instructions for performing an exorcism!

IS IT HAUNTED?

Have you ever seen or been in a place that you thought was haunted? Ghosts have been suspected of haunting all kinds of buildings. Believers usually think a haunted house is connected with a ghost or other spirit that was associated with it in life. That connection can be positive—perhaps the soul was happiest there. Or the connection can be negative—a location associated with guilt, fear, sadness, or shock. The place might even be where the soul's body died. And a ghost may haunt people if it thinks they're responsible for its death, or so some believe.

In tales of hauntings, ghosts can appear as see-through visions or dark shadows. They might not be able to be seen but they may move things. They might scream, laugh, or even make music.

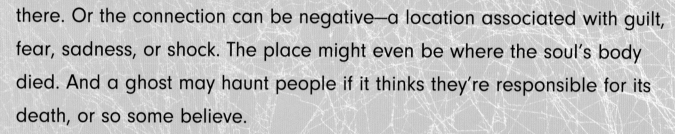

CHINESE GHOST LORE

Ghosts are a major part of Chinese folklore. An ancient Chinese belief states that each person has a soul of two parts: *po* and *hun*. These two parts need each other. And in ancient lore, if a person wasn't buried properly, both parts could return and cause trouble for the living in different ways. The *po* might haunt a house, for example. The *hun* of the soul could even possess someone.

APPARITIONS

BOGEYS

SPIRITS

PHANTOMS

DIFFERENT
NAMES FOR
GHOSTS

PHANTASMS

SPECTERS

SPOOKS

SHADOWS

SHADES

Which of these names for ghosts have you heard of?

IT'S A FACT!

In Chinese lore, the ground under the earth was the property of the gods. Before a grave could be dug, people had to "buy" land from the gods in a special ceremony.

POLTERGEISTS

Apoltergeist is a kind of ghost that isn't associated with a body. Some believe it still does a good job of making its presence known, though! The word "poltergeist" comes from the German terms *Polter* (noise) and *Geist* (spirit).

According to believers, a poltergeist is a spirit that causes physical disturbances. It makes weird or loud noises, causes objects to move unexpectedly, and breaks household items. Sometimes a poltergeist is blamed for starting fires too. Some say this spirit mainly tries to bother one person. A poltergeist's activity may stop if a stranger comes near, though, so it's hard to prove what's going on. Some believe poltergeists are spirits of the dead, while others think the strange events occur because of a living person's **psychic** energy.

DIFFERENT CULTURES, DIFFERENT SPIRITS

In Irish tales, the scream of a spirit called a banshee predicts death. Evil ghouls, or *ghūls*, appear in Arabic folklore. They lived in deserted places, like graveyards. They could change how they appeared. In Germany, kobolds were often helpful spirits that did chores and sang to children. But they might also hide objects or knock over things. Huli myths of Papua New Guinea describe nature spirits called *dama dagenda*. They give nosebleeds and sores to people who travel through their land.

Welsh people told of a spirit somewhat like
the spooky banshee of the Irish. It was called
Gwrach y Rhibyn (Witch of Rhibyn).

IT'S A FACT!

Folklore is the name for the beliefs, tales, songs, and other
traditions that a culture passes down. Ghosts, poltergeists, and
other spirits are part of folklore.

WHAT HAPPENED IN AMITYVILLE?

In 1974, six members of the DeFeo family were shot and killed in their home in Amityville, New York. The murderer was later discovered to be Ronald DeFeo Jr., the eldest son.

The DeFeo house was sold the next year to George and Kathy Lutz. Soon after they moved in with their children, they reported some horrors of their own. They claimed cabinet doors slammed by themselves and were ripped off hinges. They said they saw demon faces and slime dripping from the ceiling. They also said insects attacked them. They moved out after 28 days.

The tale was made into popular books and movies. Ronald DeFeo Jr.'s lawyer later admitted he and the Lutzes made up these incidents to make money. Some still believe the house is haunted, though.

BEST-SELLING BOOK

In 1977, author Jay Anson published a book about the Lutzes' experience called *The Amityville Horror: A True Story*. The book became a best seller, but it also led to people finding flaws in the supposedly true story. One researcher, Rick Moran, said he found more than 100 errors and problems with the tale of the haunted house on Long Island. Still, many people choose to believe the family's story.

The DeFeo and Lutz families lived at 112 Ocean Avenue, Amityville, New York, which is on Long Island.

IT'S A FACT!

Later owners of 112 Ocean Avenue changed its address to keep away people who were curious about the house and the events that have taken place there.

A HAUNTED CASTLE?

A 900-year-old castle in Scotland is another building that many believe is haunted. Built in the 12th century, Edinburgh Castle has survived all kinds of attacks and political struggles over the centuries. It served as a military fortress, prison, and home for royalty.

In 2001, a team of researchers and 240 volunteers performed a kind of experiment in Edinburgh Castle. The volunteers were asked to record their experiences while wandering the castle over 10 days. They were not informed about which parts of the castle were said to be haunted. Just over half said they experienced paranormal events in the areas with stories of hauntings, and more than a third reported similar experiences in areas not connected with hauntings. What conclusions would you draw?

NORMAL OR PARANORMAL?

Paranormal describes something that can't be explained by science. The prefix *para*– means "beyond" or "outside of." So what did people experience at Edinburgh Castle that could be described as outside of normal? People have reported seeing shadowy figures, sensing strangely cold spots, and feeling someone—or something—tugging on their clothes. Some have also reported hearing the sound of drums. And nothing around them indicated why these experiences might have occurred.

Some visitors to Edinburgh Castle say they've seen the ghost of a headless drummer!

IT'S A FACT!

In the 1500s and 1600s, over 300 women accused of being witches were imprisoned at Edinburgh Castle and later killed.

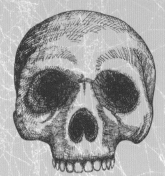

Under Paris, France, more than 6 million people are buried along around 200 miles (322 km) of dark, winding tunnels called the Paris Catacombs. How did this happen?

In the 1700s, the graveyards of Paris were becoming too full. It became a health problem. Beginning in 1785, bodies were moved from the graveyards to below the city in the dark of night. The last person was buried in the catacombs in 1860. To this day, the catacombs still hold the remains of these dead.

People can tour part of the catacombs—if they dare. Bones line the tunnels. Visitors have said they felt hands they could not see touching them. Others have sensed they were being followed. A few unfortunate visitors have felt like they were being choked!

LOST IN THE TUNNELS

One ghost story about the Paris Catacombs is especially haunting. Philibert Aspairt worked at a French hospital until he went missing in 1793. His body was finally found 11 years later—in the catacombs. It's believed he got lost in the darkness of the tunnels and died before finding a way out. His remains were found very close to an exit. Some say he haunts the catacombs one day a year, November 3, the day he went missing.

People tunneled below Paris long before the dead were buried there. They used the limestone rock beneath the city as a building material.

The Paris Catacombs were named the Paris **Municipal** Ossuary in 1786. An ossuary is a place that holds the bones of the dead.

WHITE HOUSE HAUNTINGS

Perhaps the most famous house in the United States is the White House, the home of the U.S. president. According to some, it's also the most famous haunted house!

There are accounts of First Lady Abigail Adams (above), who died in 1818, being seen doing laundry. Gardeners claimed First Lady Dolley Madison's ghost frightened them after they had been instructed to move her beloved Rose Garden. But President Abraham Lincoln (shown on the next page) is likely the most reported apparition.

Many people have said they've either seen Lincoln's ghost or felt his presence. Eleanor Roosevelt said she felt Lincoln looking over her shoulder as she worked in the Lincoln Bedroom. One story goes that British prime minister Winston Churchill stepped out of his late-night bath to see Lincoln's ghost!

THE DEMON CAT OF DC?

Another ghost story has persisted in Washington, DC, for over 100 years. It's the legend of the ghost cat! In one newspaper story, the cat, sometimes called the Demon Cat, is said to appear normal size but then balloon to the size of an elephant. Some say the ghost cat emerges before a tragedy, such as the stock market crash of 1929 and the **assassination** of President John F. Kennedy in 1963. It's been spotted at the Capitol and the White House.

Some have said they've heard the voice of David Burns while in the Oval Office. Burns was a tobacco farmer who once owned the land where the White House (above) now sits.

IT'S A FACT!

Some ghost stories relating to the White House have roots in real events, like the burning of the building by British soldiers during the War of 1812.

GHOSTS OF GETTYSBURG

Gettysburg, Pennsylvania, was the location of a bloody battle in the American Civil War (1861–1865). The Northern and Southern forces fought at Gettysburg from July 1 to July 3, 1863. The armies of the North won, but more than 50,000 soldiers died in all. Part of the battlefield became a national cemetery, or graveyard. Many people visit Gettysburg today to learn about the battle. Some are also curious about reports of Gettysburg being haunted.

So many Gettysburg buildings and structures are said to be haunted that ghost tours are a big business there. Strange sounds, sights, and even smells have been reported at the Sachs Covered Bridge, which was used by both sides in the war. The ghost of a soldier from Texas was spotted on the battlefield in a place called Devil's Den.

ODD ORBS

Some people who take pictures around Gettysburg and other supposedly haunted places find glowing orbs, or spheres, in their images. A few believe these round lights captured in photographs are hovering ghosts. The orbs are invisible to the human eye and only seen in photos. So, what's going on? Camera flashes are known to create orbs in images when they reflect off dust, rain, or similar bits in the air. But some think this doesn't explain all photographed orbs.

THE ANGLE

Some think Gettysburg is haunted because so many soldiers lost their lives there in a terrible way.

Ghost tours aren't allowed on the battlefield in Gettysburg, out of respect for the dead.

GHOST HUNTERS

Some people hunt ghosts! They go to locations said to be haunted and hope to find hard evidence that spirits actually exist. First, these ghost hunters need to make sure they're not breaking the law by exploring these places. It's illegal to be on private property without permission.

Ghost hunters must choose a time to investigate. Some people call the hours between 9 p.m. and 6 a.m. the psychic hours and believe ghosts are most likely to show themselves during this time. Certain ghosts might be said to appear at times that were special to them in life.

Just seeing a ghost isn't enough for most ghost hunters. They want to be able to capture that ghost in a photograph or on video to convince others of ghosts' existence.

GHOSTLY EQUIPMENT

Some ghost hunters use more than cameras in their explorations. They use audio recorders to catch any spooky voices or sounds and video recorders to capture weird movements. Some use **infrared** thermometers to measure temperature changes. A sudden cold spot that's not near a window or air conditioner might mean a ghost or other spirit has appeared. Another piece of ghost-detecting equipment is an **electromagnetic** field (EMF) meter. It can detect changes in electrical charges, which some think means a spirit's presence.

It can be a good idea for a ghost hunter to use a headlamp so they can have their hands free to use other ghost-spotting tools, like this EMF meter.

People can buy ghost-hunting apps for smartphones!

Ghost hunters spend time walking around an area to get to know the space. They may set up equipment like video cameras. Then they get to work. They write down anything that seems unusual. They may note strange feelings or emotions too, in case a spirit is causing these reactions. Sometimes ghost hunters ask questions aloud, in case spirits are listening and willing to speak.

Many ghost hunters make a timeline. The sound of footsteps on the stairs at 1 a.m., for example, can be discussed later with a ghost hunter's partner. If everyone hears it and notes it, that might be evidence that something strange is happening. And perhaps it happens at the same time each night. After the hunt, some ghost hunters suggest asking the spirits they're investigating not to follow them home.

PSEUDOSCIENCE

Some people label ghost hunting and other kinds of paranormal investigating as pseudoscience. That means they seem like science because they use similar methods, but they don't prove anything based in real science. For example, ghost hunters use scientific instruments like infrared thermometers and EMF meters, but there's no proof that data they collect is connected to ghosts or other spirits. Other kinds of pseudoscience are astrology and UFOlogy (the study of unidentified flying objects).

Some companies offer ghost-hunting adventures. This is a safe way to experience what real ghost hunters do.

IT'S A FACT!

Ghost hunters have been arrested for **trespassing** in graveyards and buildings.

EVIDENCE AND EXPLANATIONS

Some people claim to have seen ghosts many times. Ghost **skeptics** have some explanations for that. Seeing objects move might be linked to the brain. When certain parts of the brain are damaged, a person can have vision problems—and possibly experience a ghostly vision. People with **epilepsy** might also have a creepy feeling that someone is nearby or even hear voices. Tiredness, drugs, alcohol, and poor lighting are more explanations for ghost sightings.

What about photographic evidence? It's possible to alter a photograph to make it look like a spirit is visible. Check out the next page to see how a double exposure combines two images into one photo. Photo-editing computer programs make changing photographs even easier. Anyone can learn how to put a "ghost" into a photo!

A SPIRIT PHOTOGRAPHER

Even in the early days of photography, some people altered images. One of the most famous "spirit photographers" was William Mumler. In the 1860s, people asked Mumler to take their picture, hoping that a loved one's image would appear in the photo as well. He often gave them photos with ghostly images that people assumed were their deceased loved ones. Mumler was accused of **fraud**, but no one ever knew for certain how he created his spirit photographs.

HOW TO MAKE A DOUBLE EXPOSURE USING FILM CAMERAS

Take a photograph with a film camera. The shutter opens and closes, exposing the film to one image.

↓

Rewind the film.

↓

Take a second photo. The same piece of film is exposed to a second image.

↓

Develop.

↓

Look at the double-exposed photo. It shows two exposures— two images—in one photo.

Spirit photographer William Mumler created this image of Mary Todd Lincoln with the ghostly shadow of her husband Abraham Lincoln behind her.

IT'S A FACT!

Some digital cameras allow the photographer to choose an image over which to produce a second exposure, so the images can be combined.

WHAT DO YOU BELIEVE?

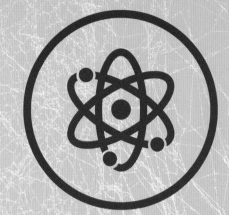

Skeptics point out that ghost hunters often find evidence, but not absolute proof that could persuade others. For example, they may take a photograph with a weird blur of light or record an odd creaking sound. These things, even together, don't mean a ghost was present. You can probably think of explanations for these events.

Still, some believers in ghosts won't be convinced spirits aren't all around us. Science can't explain everything, they say. For some, it's comforting to think a loved one is near and that there's life after death. So people will continue to tell their ghost stories. And while there isn't proof that ghosts exist, there isn't proof they don't exist. It's time to decide: What do you believe?

SORTING FACT FROM FICTION

Some ghost hunters and other investigators of the paranormal acknowledge that much paranormal activity isn't real. They find themselves debunking stories, which means proving them to be false. They still hope to find proof, though. Often, when people don't know the answer to a question, their mind searches for a way to explain it. That may be where some ghost tales come from. Still, for people who truly believe they've seen a ghost, no further explanation is needed!

If you think you'll see ghosts in a house like this, you're more likely to!

Many ideas about ghosts and spirits come from movies like *Ghostbusters* and TV shows like *Ghost Hunters* and *Scooby-Doo.*

GLOSSARY

assassination: the act of killing someone, especially a public figure

Babylonian: having to do with an ancient country in western Asia

culture: the beliefs and ways of life of a group of people

electromagnetic: the magnetic field that a current of electricity produces

epilepsy: a brain disorder that can cause people to lose consciousness and to have uncontrolled body movements

fraud: the crime of doing something in a dishonest way in order to take something of value from another person

infrared: producing invisible rays of light that are longer than rays that produce red light

municipal: having to do with the government of a town, city, or region

psychic: believed to have supernatural abilities or features

skeptic: someone who has doubt or disbelief about a certain subject

trespass: to go onto someone's land unlawfully

FOR MORE INFORMATION

Books

Boutland, Craig. *Ghoulish Ghosts*. Minneapolis, MN: Lerner Publications, 2019.

Hollihan, Kerrie Logan. *Ghosts Unveiled!* New York, NY: Abrams Books for Young Readers, 2020.

Oachs, Emily Rose. *Ghosts*. Minneapolis, MN: Bellwether Media, 2019.

Websites
Are Ghosts Real?
kids.tpl.ca/wonders/682
Before you decide what you believe, read this summary of the ghost debate.

White House Ghost Stories
www.whitehousehistory.org/press-room-old/white-house-ghost-stories
Read more creepy tales about other spirits in the White House.

Publisher's note to educators and parents: Our editors have carefully reviewed these websites to ensure that they are suitable for students. Many websites change frequently, however, and we cannot guarantee that a site's future contents will continue meet our high standards and educational value. Be advised that students showed be clearly supervised whenever they access the internet.

INDEX